P9-CFJ-830

$5.95

Dorrie and the Dreamyard Monsters

Story and Pictures by
PATRICIA COOMBS

Dorrie, the little witch, and everyone else in Witchville were having nightmares. So Dorrie's mother decided to conjure up the Dream Witch, and see what could be done about it.

But, in her headlong way, the Big Witch rushed off to the conjuring at Witches' Meadow, leaving behind a mix-up of cloaks and potions that only a quick-witted little witch like Dorrie could straighten out.

For Dorrie and her cat Gink soon found themselves in the Dreamyard, surrounded by an unruly mob of nightmare monsters. How Dorrie subdued them leads to the satisfying conclusion of another delightful story by the popular author-artist.

0610

Dorrie and the Dreamyard Monsters

by Patricia Coombs

CARNEGIE LIBRARY
LIVINGSTONE COLLEGE
SALISBURY, N. C. 28144

Lothrop, Lee & Shepard Company ✶ New York

A Division of William Morrow & Co., Inc.

Other books by Patricia Coombs

Dorrie and the Amazing Magic Elixir

Dorrie and the Birthday Eggs

Dorrie and the Blue Witch

Dorrie and the Fortune Teller

Dorrie and the Goblin

Dorrie and the Halloween Plot

Dorrie and the Haunted House

Dorrie and the Weather-Box

Dorrie and the Witch Doctor

Dorrie and the Witch's Imp

Dorrie and the Wizard's Spell

Lisa and the Grompet

The Magic Pot

Molly Mullett

Mouse Café

Copyright © 1977 by Patricia Coombs. All rights reserved. No part of this book may be reproduced or utilized in any form or by any means, electronic or mechanical, including photocopying, recording or by any information storage and retrieval system, without permission in writing from the Publisher. Inquiries should be addressed to Lothrop, Lee & Shepard Company, 105 Madison Ave., New York, N. Y. 10016. Printed in the United States of America.

Library of Congress Cataloging in Publication Data

Coombs, Patricia.
  Dorrie and the dreamyard monsters.

  SUMMARY: After Dorrie rescues the Dream Witch from imprisonment by the Dreamyard monsters, pleasant dreams replace the nightmares of the residents of Witchville.
  [1. Witches—Fiction] I. Title.
PZ7.C7813Djd   [Fic]   77-1373
ISBN 0-688-41807-4
ISBN 0-688-51807-9 lib. bdg.

J 813.54
C 775

For Jim
who made room in the closet.

105519

This is Dorrie. She is a witch. A little witch. Her hat is always on crooked and her socks never match. She lives in a tall, dark house with her mother, the Big Witch, and Cook. Wherever Dorrie goes, her black cat Gink goes with her.

One afternoon Dorrie went into the kitchen. Cook was making a cup of tea and mumbling to herself.

"Cook," said Dorrie, "when will . . ."

"I don't know!" shouted Cook. "Don't bother me!"

"Oh," said Dorrie. "You must have had more nightmares last night. Me, too."

Cook frowned at the tea. "I dreamed I was a cookie, and a monster with big feet stepped on me. I was nothing but crumbs. Nightmares, bad dreams, and now sleep walking! The Big Witch found Squig standing in the pond this morning. And Mr. Obs was stuck in a tree. He dreamed a purple monster was after him. None of the spells has worked. And the nightmares are getting worse."

A black shadow whizzed across the window.

"Mother's home from the meeting," said Dorrie. "I bet she found out another way to get rid of the nightmares."

"I bet she forgot the vanilla," grumbled Cook. "I hope so. I never want to see another cookie."

Dorrie and Gink ran into the hall and up the stairs. The Big Witch was running, her black cloak flapping. She opened the door that led up to the secret room.

"Mother, wait!" said Dorrie. "What are you going to do? Have you got a new spell?"

"Tonight, in Witches' Meadow," said the Big Witch, "we will have a conjuring. I've been chosen to be the conjuror and to mix a special potion. I must hurry. Witchville hasn't had a conjuring for years. I have to go early and practice."

"Who are you going to conjure up?" said Dorrie.

"The Dream Witch. She's in charge of the Dreamyard. The potion is for her. She uses it to keep dreams from turning into nightmares." The Big Witch frowned. "Since our spells haven't worked, we think the Dream Witch has run out of potion."

"I'll help," said Dorrie.

"All right," said the Big Witch. "But you must do exactly as I say. And be quick. The conjuring must be done before the moon reaches the top of the Town Tower. If it isn't done by then, we have to wait a whole year before we can do it again."

"A whole year of nightmares?" said Dorrie.

The Big Witch nodded and shuddered.

Up, up, up the stairs they went to the little secret room at the top of the tower.

"Here," said the Big Witch. "Put my cloak over there with my conjuring cloak. Carefully! Cook's vanilla is in the pocket. Now, find me the spoon with the moon on the handle."

The Big Witch opened the Book of Magic. She muttered and mumbled as she turned the pages. Then she covered the window so the room was dark. She began measuring out magic and pouring it into the cauldron.

Slowly the magic began to bubble and shine. The Big Witch stirred and stirred, whispering magic words.

"I had a nightmare, too," said Dorrie, "a big . . ."

"SHHH!" hissed the Big Witch. "Quick, the jar of purple crystals!"

Dorrie handed the Big Witch the jar. The Big Witch sprinkled a spoonful into the cauldron. Green flames flickered across the magic.

"Now, the box of moth wings! Hurry!"

Dorrie looked around. "It isn't here."

"Stir!" whispered the Big Witch. "I'll get it."

Dorrie stirred and stirred. The Big Witch pulled her head out of the closet. "I found it!" She took the spoon from Dorrie and stirred in some of the powder from the box. Blue flames flickered over the magic and faded away.

The Big Witch waved her hands in the air over the cauldron, making magic signs.

"There," said the Big Witch. "It's all done. Now get me a bottle."

Dorrie held the bottle while the Big Witch poured the potion into it.

"I'll leave it right here in my cloak pocket. It will cool while I get ready. I must hurry or I won't have time to practice!"

Down, down, down the stairs they went.

"I'll be ready in a minute," said Dorrie.

"NO, NO!" cried the Big Witch. "Conjurings are dangerous! Only grown-ups can come. Go eat supper and GO TO BED. I'll come home as soon as it's over. I'll take you back with me to Witches' Meadow and we'll have a bonfire."

"I want to go with you," said Dorrie. "I'll . . ."

"Don't pester me! It's getting late. Eat your bed! Go to supper!" The Big Witch swished into her room and slammed the door.

Dorrie sighed. Down, down, down the stairs she went, and Gink went with her. They went into the kitchen. Cook was in her room getting ready. They ate their supper. The Big Witch came running down from the tower, her cloak flapping.

"Go right to bed!" cried the Big Witch. "And DON'T TURN ON YOUR LIGHT. All of Witchville must be dark for the conjuring!"

With a swirl and a swish, a rush and a slam, Cook and the Big Witch were gone. Dorrie and Gink were alone.

Dorrie put the dishes in the sink. She and Gink climbed slowly up the stairs. Dorrie put on her nightgown.

"I can't sleep," said Dorrie. "It's too dark and too quiet." She looked out the window. She couldn't see anything. The house creaked. Dorrie went into the hall. She stopped. The door to the tower was open.

"Hmmm," said Dorrie. "Mother left in such a hurry she forgot to close it. I bet we can see Witches' Meadow from up there. Come on, Gink."

Up, up, up the stairs they went. The cauldron was still shining from the magic. A faint glow filled the little room. Bats squeaked in the shadows. Dorrie shivered.

"There's Mother's cloak. That will keep me warm while we watch the conjuring." Dorrie wrapped the big black cloak around her. Something bumped against her leg. She reached into the pocket and pulled out a bottle.

"Oh," said Dorrie. "Cook's vanilla." She looked closer. The bottle was glowing like the cauldron.

"Vanilla doesn't glow. Mother took the wrong cloak! She's got the vanilla and I've got the potion for the Dream Witch! Come on, Gink!"

Down, down, down the stairs they ran, out the door and across the yard. Down the road and across the fields they ran. They scrambled over a wall, and through the trees at the edge of Witches' Meadow.

The moon was just coming up. All the witches and wizards were lying in a circle in the middle of the meadow, with their toes pointing out. The Big Witch stood in the center, waving her arms and chanting. The bottle of vanilla was sitting on top of the Moon Stone. Slowly the Big Witch sank to the ground.

"Oh, no" said Dorrie. "We're too late!" All at once Dorrie felt herself flying through the air and spinning around and around and around. There was a thump and a bump. They stopped.

They sat up. There was a strange purple light. Couches and beds and mirrors and doors and ladders and sinks were piled up all around them.

"Hmm," said Dorrie. "This isn't Witches' Meadow. What a mess! It looks like some kind of junkyard."

Gink hissed. His fur stood on end. Dorrie looked behind her. Big shadowy shapes were climbing over couches and chairs, creeping around sinks and stoves. They yawned huge yawns. Wings flapped. Teeth and claws shone in the strange light. They came nearer and nearer.

"Monsters!" yelled Dorrie. She and Gink began to run. They ran around pianos and tables, jumped over beds, and scrambled between chairs.

The shadow of flapping wings moved over them, closer and closer. Huge paws reached out. Dorrie and Gink ducked behind a door. Paws grabbed the door and tossed it away. They slid under a bed. Paws grabbed the bed and tossed it away. The monsters began growling and roaring, louder and louder.

Dorrie and Gink scrambled up over a pile of stuff.

"Look, Gink, a swing! I've got an idea. Come on!"

As paws reached out to grab them, Dorrie jumped on the swing with Gink. She began to swing, higher and higher, right over the heads of the monsters.

The monsters stopped. They looked up at Dorrie and Gink. They looked at each other. They scratched their heads. They came closer.

When she was swinging high enough to be out of reach of the monsters, Dorrie reached into the cloak pocket. She pulled out the bottle of potion.

"I hope this works," said Dorrie. "If it doesn't I think we're in trouble." As they swung out high over the monsters, Dorrie threw the potion over them.

There was a flash of light and a fizz. The growls turned to purrs and snuffling whispers. All around her, the monsters crawled, bobbing their heads and smiling.

Dorrie and Gink climbed out of the swing. Arms and paws wrapped all around them.

"Phew," said Dorrie. "What a nightmare! A nightmare! These are nightmare monsters. And all this stuff. We're in the Dreamyard! Mother conjured us away by mistake. We've got to hurry and find the Dream Witch!"

Back through the Dreamyard they went. The monsters followed at Dorrie's heels, tumbling all over themselves and falling into heaps. They began pushing and shoving, trying to stay close to her.

"Stop that!" yelled Dorrie. "Stay in line and stay behind me." With a flurry of wings and arms and legs and tails, they made a line.

Dorrie looked all over the Dreamyard. She couldn't find the Dream Witch. She stopped. The monsters all bumped into each other and fell in a big heap. She looked at the monsters and frowned.

"I bet you know where she is," said Dorrie. "Show me. Right now!"

The monsters all frowned and groaned and shook their heads. They began roaring and howling.

"Stop that noise!" said Dorrie. "Sit!" The monsters stopped their noise. They sat in a big circle around Dorrie and Gink. Dorrie pointed to the smallest monster. "You," said Dorrie, "show me where the Dream Witch is. And hurry up!"

CARNEGIE LIBRARY
LIVINGSTONE COLLEGE
SALISBURY, N. C. 28144

The smallest monster got up. He trotted off. They all followed him. In and out, over and under, around and around the Dreamyard they went. The monster stopped in front of a bunch of clocks. He pointed to one, then shook his head. He pointed to another. And another.

"You put the Dream Witch in a clock?" said Dorrie.

The monsters nodded.

"And you don't remember which one?" The monsters shook their heads.

"Well, find out!" said Dorrie.

At that, the monsters leaped into the air and landed on the clocks, knocking them all over. As the biggest clock crashed, the door flew open. Up sat a silvery witch with her hat knocked sideways. The monsters roared and made a leap for her.

"Stop that! Sit!" said Dorrie. They stopped. They sat.

The silvery witch climbed out of the clock. She fixed her hat. She smiled at Dorrie.

"I am the Dream Witch," she said. "Thank you for saving me. I was afraid I was going to be locked in that clock forever." She frowned at the monsters. The monsters growled. "When I ran out of potion, these stupid monsters took over the Dreamyard. They turned everything upside down and backwards and locked me in the clock. Just wait until I get more potion. They'll be sorry!"

The monsters roared and stood up. "Quiet!" said Dorrie. "Sit!" They were quiet. They sat.

"What have you done to them?" cried the Dream Witch. "Why are they doing what you tell them to do? Are you a nightmare witch?" She turned pale.

Dorrie shook her head. "It's the potion. I threw the potion on them that the Big Witch fixed for you. She was going to conjure you into the meadow to give you the potion. But she had on the wrong cloak. I had on her conjuring cloak so I got conjured away instead. And now I've got to get home, right away. The Big Witch is going to be very upset."

"Oh, no!" cried the Dream Witch. "I can only leave the Dreamyard for a few seconds during a conjuring. If you go, I'll be left here alone with the monsters. They'll lock me up again. The nightmares will go on forever!"

The monsters began growling and howling and pawing the air.

"Hush!" said Dorrie. The monsters hushed. "I know. I'll take the monsters back with me. We'll mix up more potion for you and have another conjuring."

"And I can get the monsters when I get the potion!" said the Dream Witch.

"Oh, I hope there's time for another conjuring," said Dorrie. "If there isn't, Witchville will be full of nightmare monsters for a whole year. Mother would be very upset."

The Dream Witch looked up at the moon. She smiled. "I'll get you back in time. But you must promise that the potion will be the same kind you used on these monsters. The old potion just scared them and they hid. I want them to do what I tell them. And the first thing I'll tell them is to clean up the Dreamyard."

The monsters howled and groaned.

"Oh hush, monsters," said Dorrie. Then she turned to the Dream Witch. "I promise the potion will be the same."

The Dream Witch led Dorrie to a big silvery bathtub.

"Get in, and close your eyes. And don't open them until you feel a thump."

Dorrie and Gink climbed in. The monsters piled themselves all around and over them. They all closed their eyes.

The Dream Witch began humming. They began spinning. Faster and faster and faster they spun. The humming stopped. There was a thump, and a bump. Dorrie and Gink and the monsters rolled across the grass and sat up.

"We're back in the meadow!" said Dorrie.

Cook and all the witches and wizards opened their eyes and sat up. They saw the monsters, and ran yelling and shrieking out of the meadow.

The Big Witch stuck her head out from behind the Moon Stone. She blinked. "I'm dreaming! Nightmares! Monsters! And vanilla. I smell vanilla. Oh, we've all been turned into cookies!" She pinched herself. "Ouch!" said the Big Witch.

"Mother!" said Dorrie. "You're awake. The conjuring didn't work. You had the wrong cloak, the one with the vanilla in it. You conjured me away instead of conjuring up the Dream Witch. Hurry, we have to do it all over again."

The Big Witch and Dorrie and Gink leaped on the broomstick. "Come on, monsters," called Dorrie. "Follow us."

Over the dark fields and houses they flew. The monsters flew along behind them. They all landed in the yard and hurried up to the secret room.

Dorrie and the Big Witch quickly measured and mixed and stirred. "Something about our potion was different from the recipe," said Dorrie. "We have to make it just like we did before."

"Everything looks the same to me," said the Big Witch. "Now, the moth wings!"

Dorrie picked up the box. She looked at it. She held it up for the Big Witch to see.

"Mouthwash!" whispered the Big Witch. "We used mouthwash instead of moth wings. We mixed up a love potion. No wonder the monsters follow you around. They love you!"

"Oh, my!" said Dorrie.

Dorrie held out a bottle and the Big Witch poured the potion into it. Then Dorrie gave the Big Witch the conjuring cloak. The Big Witch gave Dorrie her other cloak.

Down, down, down the stairs they went, and back to Witches' Meadow.

"Oh no!" cried the Big Witch. "The witches and wizards have all gone. We need at least thirteen for a conjuring. We can't do it. These nightmares will be in Witchville for a whole year!"

"Don't worry, Mother," said Dorrie. "Okay, monsters. Lie down in a big circle. Toes out, heads in, eyes closed."

Quick as a wink the monsters were lying in a circle with Dorrie and Gink. They all closed their eyes.

The Big Witch put the potion on the Moon Stone, held her arms in the air, and chanted the magic words. As she sank to the ground, there was a flash of blue light, a fizz, and a hum.

Another flash. The humming stopped. They opened their eyes and sat up. The monsters were gone, the potion was gone.

"It worked!" said Dorrie. "The Dream Witch was here!"

"No more nightmares! No more monsters!" said the Big Witch with a big smile. The smile faded. Dorrie looked around. The smallest monster was standing right behind her. He smiled and leaned his head against her.

"He kept his eyes open," said the Big Witch crossly. "And now it's too late for another conjuring. Look, the moon is over the Town Tower right now! I think I'm getting a headache."

"Don't worry, Mother," said Dorrie. "He can live in my closet. I don't mind. Gink and I are kind of used to him."

"Well," said the Big Witch, "all right. But keep him away from Cook. She'll have a fit if he gets in her kitchen!"

The Big Witch lighted the bonfire. The flames leaped higher and higher. The meadow grew bright. When the witches and wizards saw the bonfire, they came hurrying back. They crowded all around while the Big Witch told them about the mix-up with the cloaks and the potion. And Dorrie told them about the monsters and the Dreamyard, and the Dream Witch locked in the clock.

Dorrie showed them the smallest monster. She told him to bow and shake hands with everyone. And he bowed and shook hands and smiled and smiled.

The Big Witch clapped her hands. Mr. Obs took out his violin and began to play. And they all began to dance. Around and around the bonfire they danced and danced.

When the bonfire faded and the moon went down, they all flew home to bed.

Dorrie gave the small monster a hug and put him to sleep in her closet on top of her shoes. The Big Witch gave Dorrie a hug and tucked her into bed. Gink curled up at her feet.

And everyone in Witchville dreamed funny dreams that night, and laughed in their sleep. Even Cook.

Patricia Coombs

was born in Los Angeles, California, and received her B.S. and M.A. from the University of Washington. Dorrie and her cat Gink have appeared in twelve of Ms. Coombs' books and are based on her younger daughter and a cat named Dingbat. The Coombs family lives near a river in Connecticut, where they enjoy a houseful of pets, a garden, and a boat.

J 813.54
C775

105519

DATE DUE

NOV 1 '79	OCT 17 '79		
NOV 19 '79			
	NOV 26 '79		
OC 17 '84	OCT 17 '84		
NO 07 '84	OCT 22 '84		
GAYLORD			PRINTED IN U.S.A.

LIVINGSTONE COLLEGE LIBRARY

3 7255 00004 5167